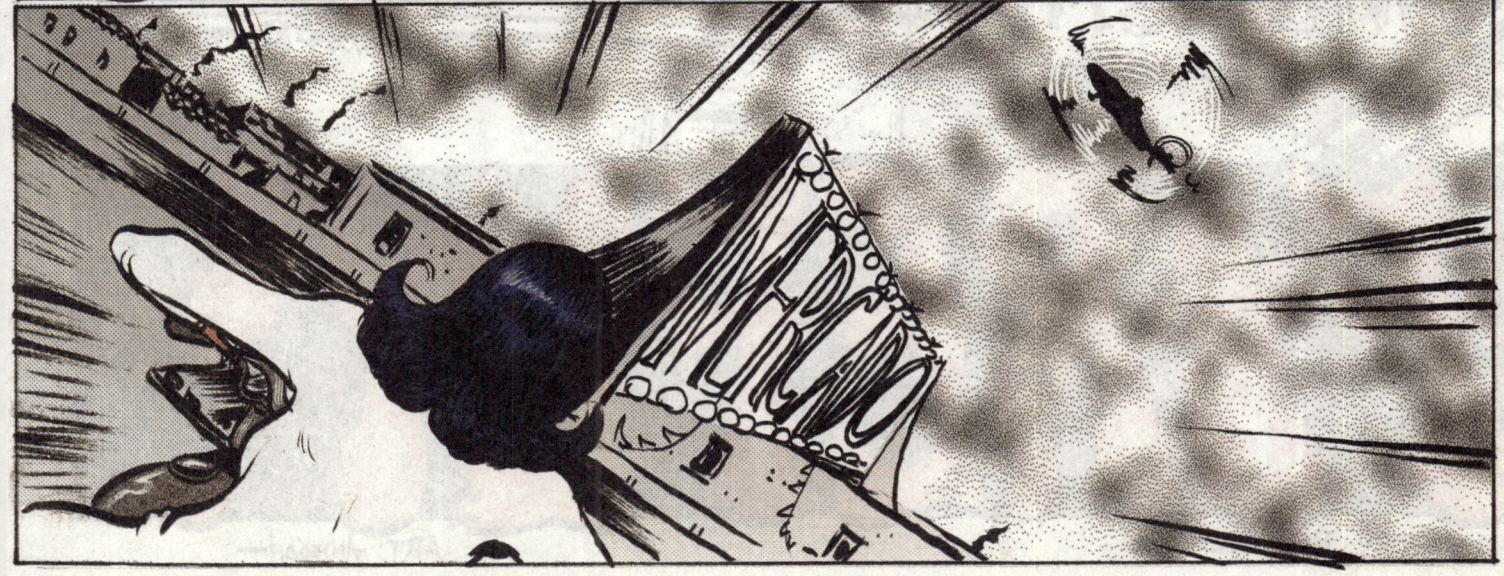

THE SICK PLAN OF **APOCALYPTICO** BECOMES CLEAR.

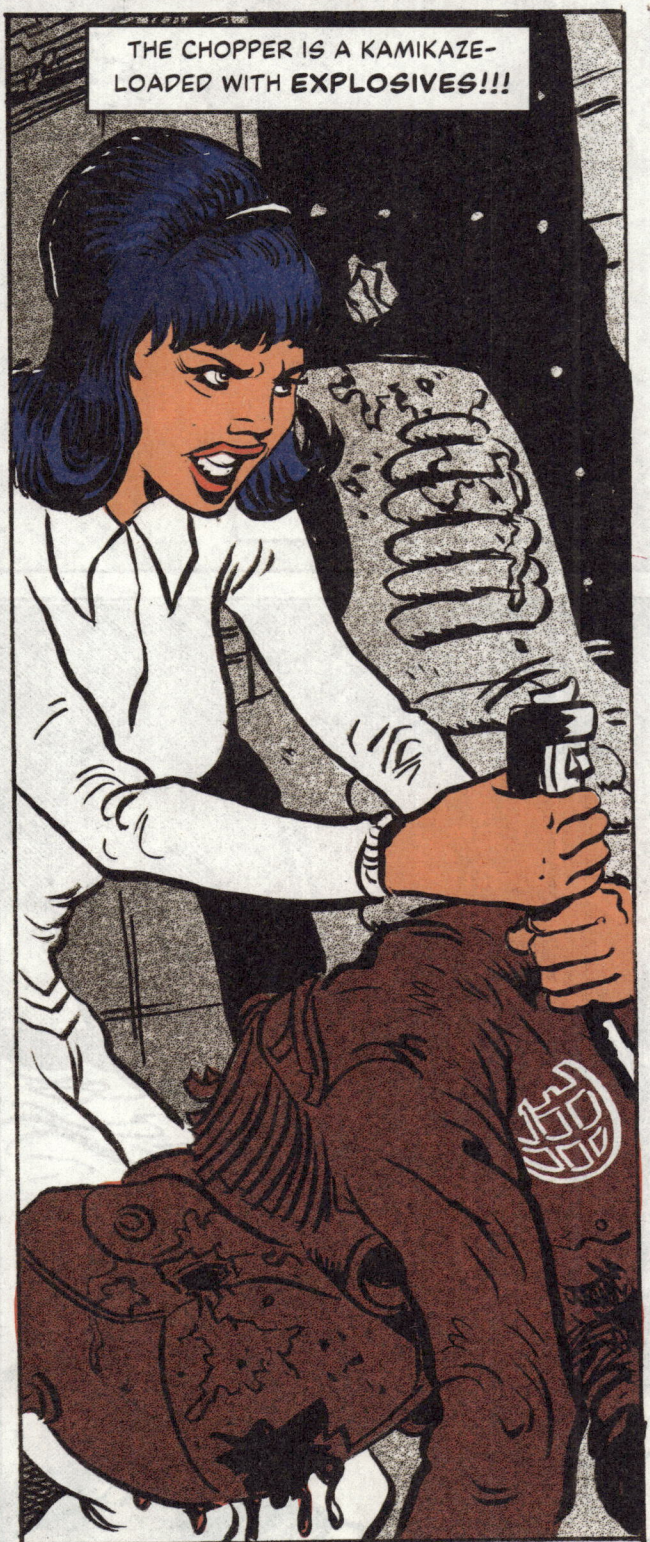

THE CHOPPER IS A KAMIKAZE- LOADED WITH **EXPLOSIVES**!!!

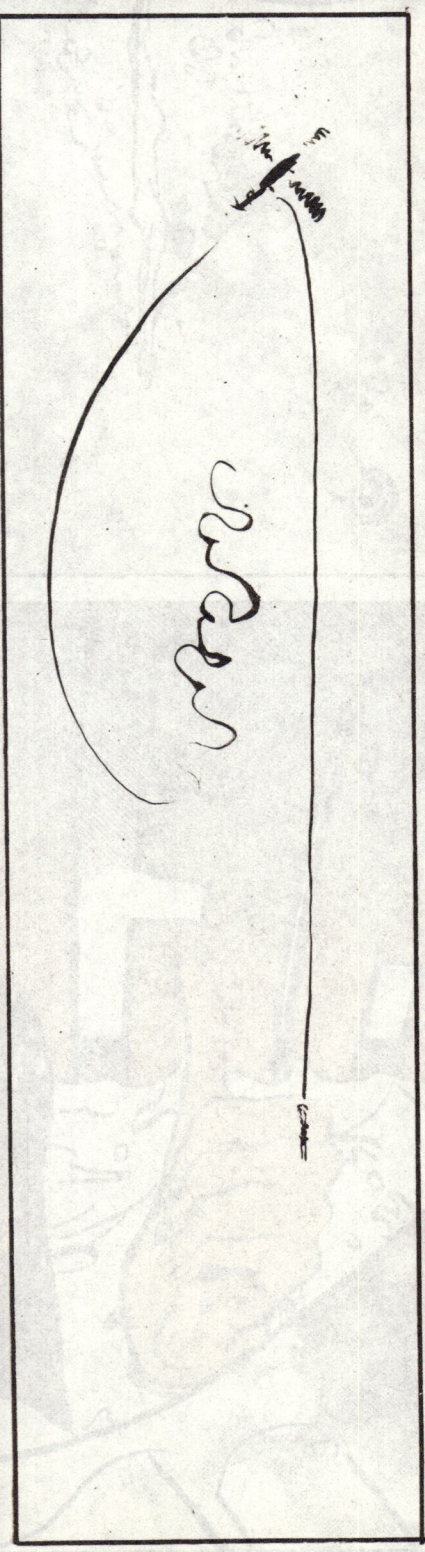

HOW MANY DIE TONIGHT?!?

ONLY THREE MEN...

...AND EACH ONE OF THEM A BASTARD.

THE END

THE POPGUN WAS BUILT FOR G.H.O.S.T. BY HOWARD HUGHES, NAMED FOR THE LOUD SOUND IT EMITS WHEN FIRED. THE LONG BARRELED HANDGUN RIVALS THE MOST POWERFUL RIFLES.

EVERY G.H.O.S.T. AGENT WEARS A WATCH OR BRACELET EMBEDDED WITH A SMALL DEVICE, TUNED TO A PARTICULAR RADIO FREQUENCY SENT FROM HEADQUARTERS. ORDERS ARE TRANSMITTED AND INTERCEPTED AS CODED PATTERNS, FELT THROUGH SMALL JOLTS OF ELECTRICITY.

MAY ZERO, LADY OF G.H.O.S.T. featuring JACK INFINITY

LOST IN THE NOWHERE ZONE
— WHERE THERE IS NO LEFT OR RIGHT!!

"IT'S BEEN A LONG TIME SINCE I GOT THIS HIGH!"

WE JOIN THE TOUGHEST WOMAN ALIVE ON AN AVERAGE AFTERNOON: TESTING THE LATEST G.H.O.S.T. TECHNOLOGY BEYOND ITS BREAKING POINT!!

'RACONTEUR' ROCKO JEROME WROTE IT!!
'BODACIOUS' BARRY TAN DREW IT!!

IT'S THE 1968 AGE OF COMICS AND YOU'RE IN FOR A WILD TIME, YOU CIRCUS ANIMALS!!

YOU... YOU SAVED ME FROM THAT... THING! EVEN WHEN I WAS ABOUT TO SHOOT YOU!

WHAT CAN I SAY, I'M SELFLESS LIKE THAT! YOU CAN RETURN THE FAVOR...

BECAUSE 'THAT LIL' DUDE I WIPED OUT HAD BUDDIES, AND SISTER, THEY AIN'T HAPPY!

AS JACK CONCENTRATES HIS CHI ON PUTTING THE WRONG THINGS RIGHT BETWEEN THE MYSTICAL AND MORTAL PLANES, THE LADY FROM G.H.O.S.T DEFENDS THE ARCANE NONCONFORMIST FROM CERTAIN DEATH!

DONNA AND CINNAMON EXPECTED TO FIGHT FIGURATIVE MONSTERS.

BEWARE THE GHOST REAPER! SCOURGE OF SPACE! DARE NOT TO DISTURB THE GHOSTS OF THE COSMOS! FOR THE REAPER SHALL CLAIM YOU! YOUR SOUL SHALL WEEP IN HELL FOR ETERNITY!

HE WILL KILL YOU

IF YOU SEE HIM YOU ARE ALREADY DEAD

3-22 JASON FOSTER

THEY DETERMINED THAT THE RIGHT COMBINATION OF RADIO WAVES AND NUCLEAR FISSION COULD OPEN - FOR A MERE FRACTION OF A SECOND -

A TEAR ...INTO THE NETHERWORLD

WRITTEN BY: ROCKO JEROME

ART BY: Adam T. Lemnah

ITALY 1968

THE TIJUANA AFFAIR

G.H.O.S.T. AGENTS

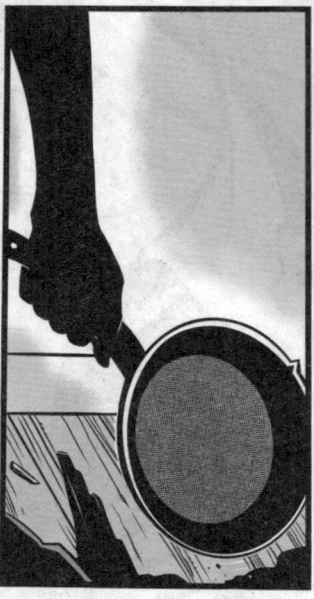

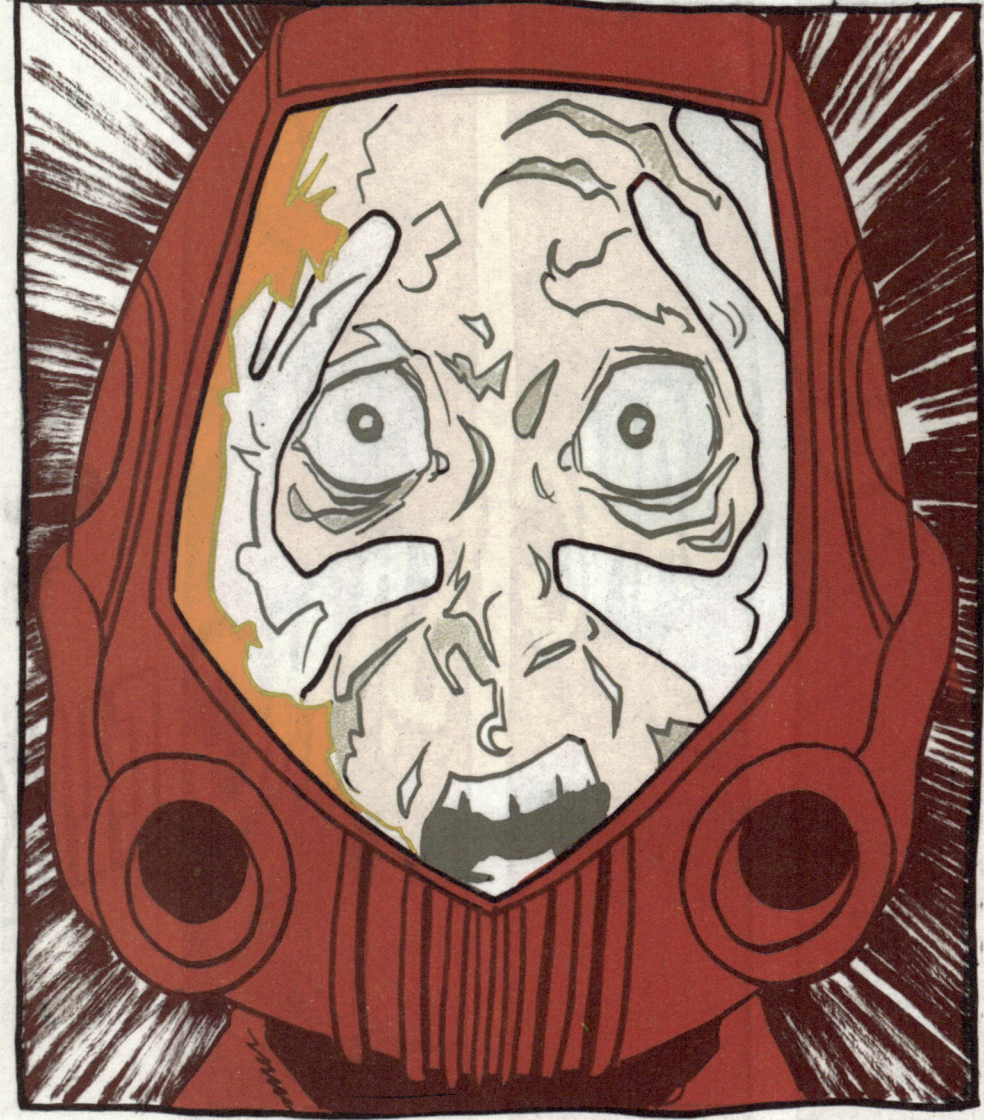

STATION DDED-87653
THE YEAR 3042.

STATION DDED-87653
THE YEAR 3042.

LONG AGO, IT WAS A THRIVING SPOT, A PLACE FOR PASSING SHIPS TO STOP, REFUEL, AND RECHARGE AS THEY CARRIED SUPPLIES ACROSS THE GALAXY.

THAT WAS UNTIL A CENTURY AGO WHEN MICRO NUCLEAR COMBUSTION MADE SUCH ROUTINE MAINTENANCE UNNECCESARY FOR ALL BUT THE MOST ARCHAIC OF SPACECRAFT. NOW THE DENIZENS ARE THE MISBEGOTTEN ANCESTORS OF THE ORIGINAL STAFF OF THE STATION. THEY CALL THEIR SHABBY HOME...

THE DEAD END

ROCKO JEROME
STORY

JOHN BURKETT
ART

COLORS BY
SHAWN COOTS
CHRIS HUMPHREYS

1973

LURED BY THE CHANCE TO AVENGE HIS MURDERED SISTER, LI ACCEPTED AN ARDUOUS MISSION FROM G.H.O.S.T.

HE SUCCEEDED, BUT AT A GREAT TOLL.

BATTERED AND SCARRED BOTH PHYSICALLY AND MENTALLY, LI RETURNS TO HIS TEMPLE.

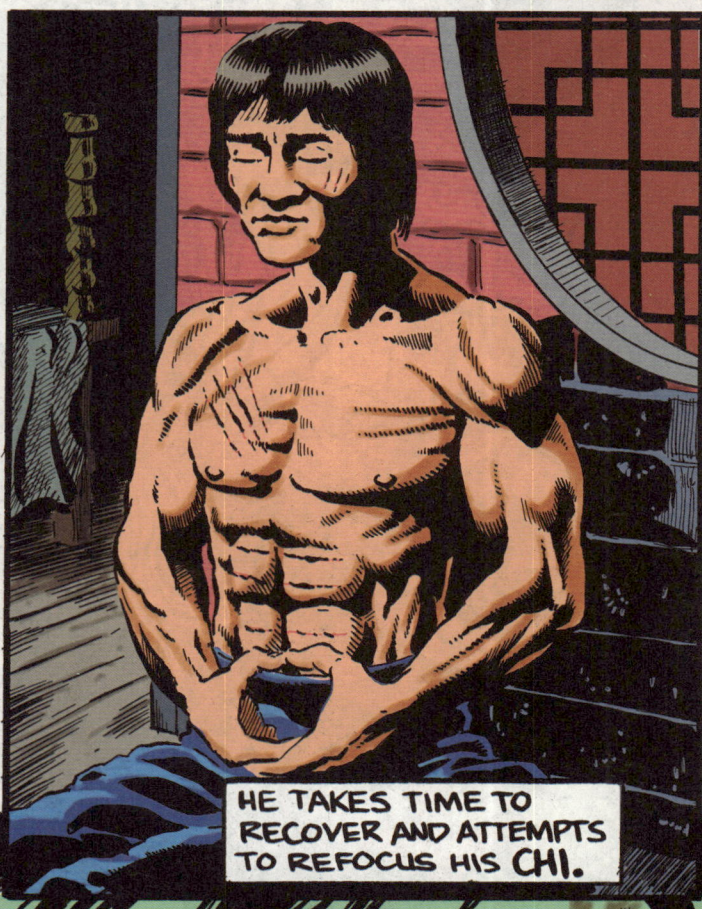

HE TAKES TIME TO RECOVER AND ATTEMPTS TO REFOCUS HIS CHI.

AS HIS MEDITATIVE FAST ENTERS ITS 100TH HOUR,...

LI REACHES A NEW PLATEAU...

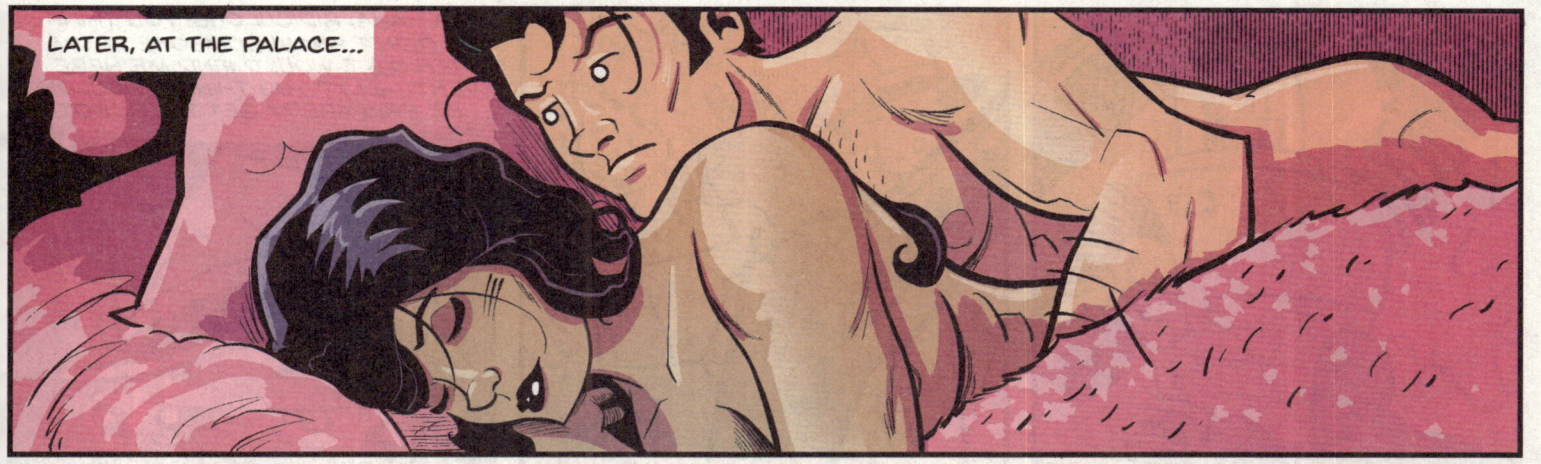

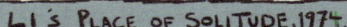

THE EGGHEADS IN OUR SCI-DIVISION THINK ALL THE ATOM BOMB TESTS OUT IN THE DESERTS OF YUCCA FLAT SOMEHOW RIPPED A HOLE IN THE TIME SPACE CONTINUUM, INTO WHAT THEY'RE CALLING... THE NETHERWORLD.

SOME VERY WEIRD THINGS HAVE BEEN CLIMBING UP OUT OF IT, AND THEY AREN'T HERE TO MAKE FRIENDS. ONE OF OUR AGENTS FOUND THAT OUT THE HARD WAY.*

*SEE GHOST AGENTS #2... IF YOU CAN FIND IT!

SCI-DIVISION BUILT A CONTRAPTION THAT WILL SHUT THE HOLE, OR RIFT, OR WHATEVER.

FIST BUMP

SOMETHING ABOUT THE RIFT IS MAKING GRAVITY WEIRD AROUND THAT AREA, TOO. GUNS ARE USELESS IN ABOUT A TEN MILE RADIUS. THAT'S WHY WE NEED YOUR... EXPERTISE. YOU AND ANNA WILL DIVE IN, BUT MAY NOT EVEN NEED YOUR PARACHUTES.

The artists in order of first appearance:

SAM J. ROYALE
@SamJRoyale, LinkTr.ee/SamJRoyale
Title logo and post-1965 GHOST logo, seen throughout

BARRY TAN
@Barry_Tan
Cover, Lost In The Nowhere Zone, The Tijuana Affair 1, slight return in The Tijuana Affair 2

CHRIS FASON
@FasonArt
Inside Front Cover, Flaming Sun

CHRIS ANDERSON
@ChrisAndersonComics, ChrisAndersonComics.com
Firefly (Both versions), The Tijuana Affair 2, Terror In The Sky

CRAIG CK
@Dull_Pen
Popgun

BEN PERKINS
@BrattyBen
Riders Howling In The Moonlight, Acid Reign

JASON FOSTER
@JasonVGFosterArt
Beware the GHOST Reaper!!!

ADAM LEMNAH
@AdamLemnah
Into Nowhere!!

CHRISTIAN J. MEESEY
@Meesimo
BOOOOM!, Edge of Reality

JACK MAXWELL
Pre-1965 GHOST logo (Seen in The Tijuana Affair)

JOHN BURKETT
@JohnBurkettStudio, JohnBurkett.SubStack.com
The Dead End, Li's Turmoil

CHRIS HUMPHREYS and SHAWN COOTS
@TopherPhotos/@CootsDaddy
The Dead End colors

DAVE PRAETORIUS
@RedEyeDraws, RedEyeDraws.com
Clutch Quartermain Lost In The Netherworld 1

DAVE GROM
@Uncle_Atomic_Press
Clutch Quartermain Lost In The Netherworld 2

DANNY NICHOLAS
@Danny_Nicholas_Jo
Men From GHOST pencils

PETER HENSEL
@TheTruGalacticus
Men From GHOST colors

MIGUEL GALINDO
@Galindo_Cartones
Donna vs The Masked Man

RICK LOPEZ
@DoomDazed
Clutch Quartermain Lost In The Netherworld 3

TONY FERO
@BigTony308
Clutch Quartermain Lost In The Netherworld 4

I want to thank all these guys for being a part of this thing. I hope their excellent work here gets them more and better paying opportunities.

Despite loving them all my life, I never even dreamed of having any role in making comics until I fell in with this crew. My gratitude is immense and eternal.

The first comic book I ever got off a spinner rack included the art of the legendary Ken Landgraf. Here, his work appears on the following pages of the first comic book I've been involved in truly mass-producing. I just asked him to draw Donna and Li fighting monsters from the Netherworld and let him rip. Keeping it in the GHOST Agents family, it's colored by Meesimo.

Thanks to **Eli Schwab** for being my partner on this ongoing project. We challenge each other to challenge ourselves.

Rocko Jerome
Writer and Producer of GHOST Agents

This book was made possible by the generosity of **Doug Schwab** and **Craig CK**.